BEAR ABOUT TOWN

Written by Stella Blackstone
Illustrated by Debbie Harter

TED SMART

Bear goes to town every day.

He likes to
walk all the way.

On Monday,
he goes to the bakery.

GRANDMA'S
BAKERY

On Tuesday,
he goes for a swim.

SPLASH ALLEY POOL

On Wednesday,
he watches a film.

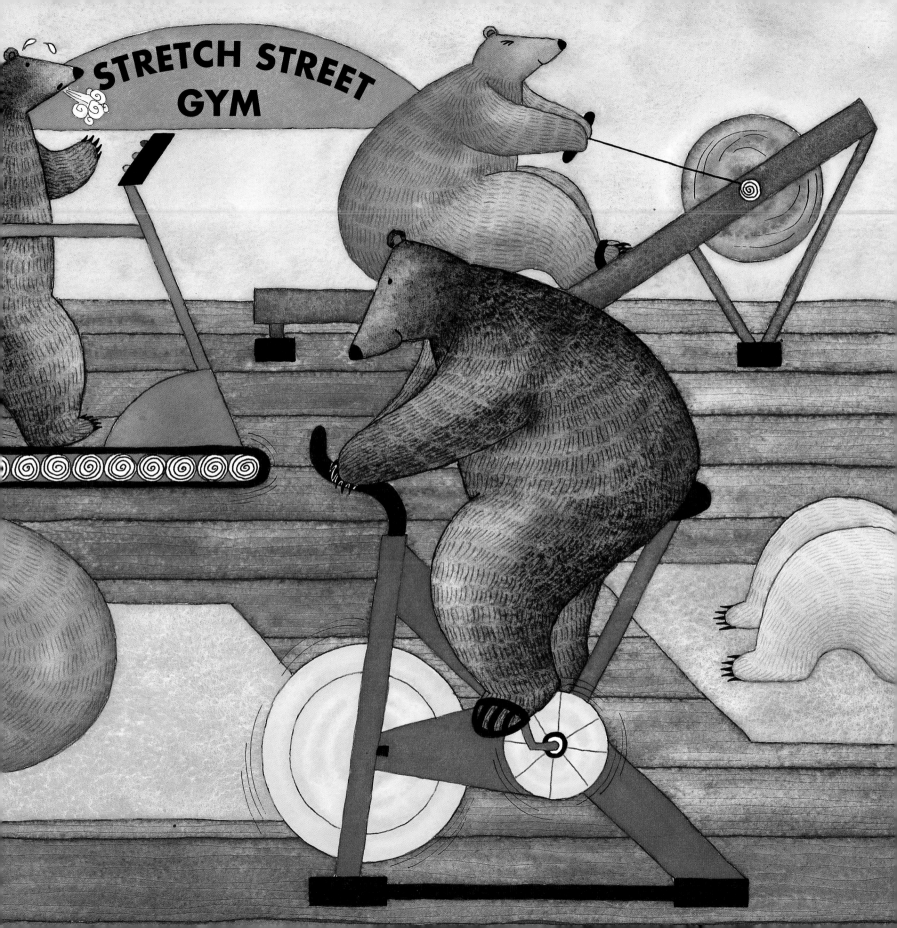

On Friday,
he goes to the toyshop.

TIP-TOP
TOYSHOP

On Saturday, he strolls through the park.

SUNNY PARK

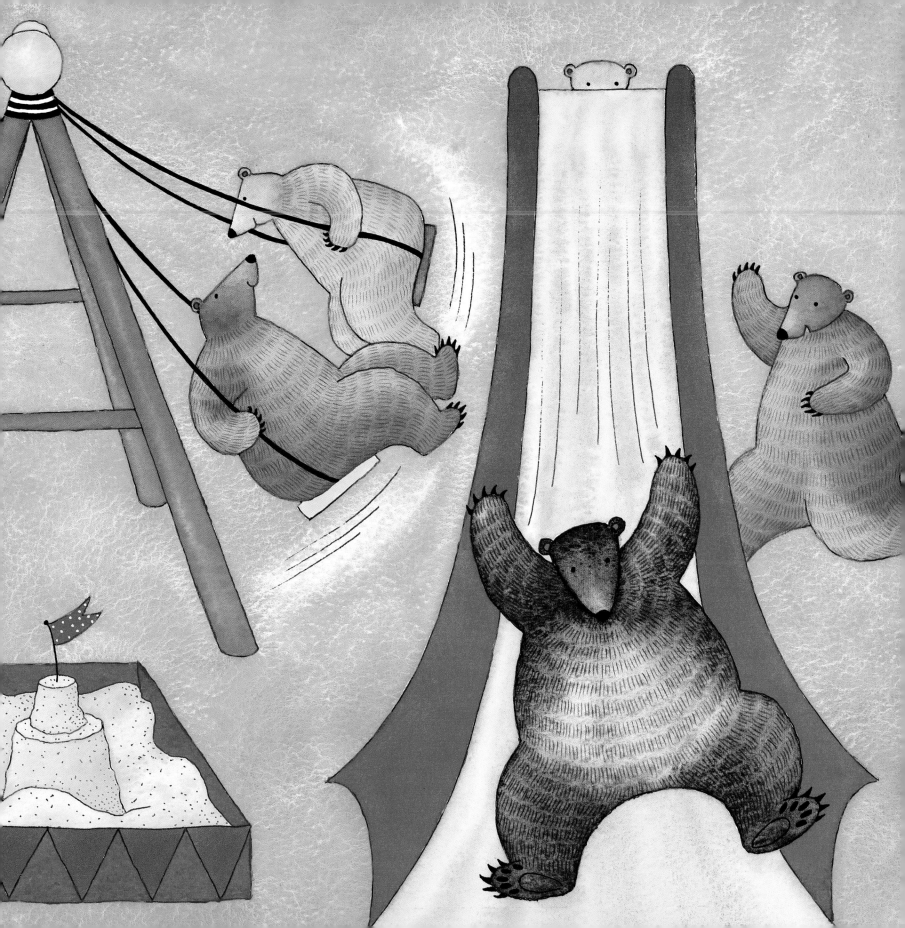

And plays with his friends until dark.

To Annabel and Dominic — S.B.
To Rosemary, John, Evelyn, Richard,
Rosie and Mary — D.H.

Barefoot Books Ltd
PO Box 95
Kingswood
Bristol
BS30 5BH

This edition produced for The Book People Ltd,
Hall Wood Avenue, Haydock, St Helens WA11 9UL
First published in Great Britain in 2000 by Barefoot Books Ltd,

This book was typeset in Futura
The illustrations were prepared in watercolour, pen and ink
and crayon on thick watercolour paper

Graphic design by Polka. Creation, Bath
Colour separation by Grafiscan, Verona
Printed and bound in Singapore by Tien Wah Press (Pte) Ltd

This book has been printed on 100% acid-free paper

ISBN 1 902283 69 4

British Cataloguing-in-Publication Data: a catalogue record for
this book is available from the British Library

1 3 5 7 9 8 6 4 2